THE

WHITE

VEENA

AKSHEEYA

THE WHITE VEENA © 2025 Aksheeya Suresh

Published by Graveside Press
graveside-press.com

Editing: Kelley York
Cover Illustration: Braden at Illumax Art – illumax.art
Cover design: Sleepy Fox Studio – sleepyfoxstudio.net
Interior Formatting: Sleepy Fox Studio – sleepyfoxstudio.net

eBook 978-1-964952-63-5
Paperback 978-1-964952-62-8

No part of this book has been created using Generative AI.

GRAVESIDE ※ PRESS

For a list of potentially triggering content,
please skip to page 34.

LAST YEAR, I MOVED to Thanjavur, a quaint and cultural temple town in South India. The town was once the cradle of an ancient Tamil dynasty stretching from the flowing Ganges down to the tip of the Indian subcontinent. These days, it is a tourist stop for God-loving pilgrims to marvel at the astounding architecture, gobble steaming *idlis*[1], sip filter *kaapis*[2], and buy dancing doll souvenirs. Sometimes, they pause on their journey and almost hear the hymns in the hot wind. A melodious whisper in the breeze sings of the town's glorious past, its kings and their conquests over land and sea, seeping into the spicy food and pooling within the laps of ancestral artisans. I was on a quest for one such artisan who could possibly be the subject of my latest story.

---

1. **idlis:** Steamed rice cakes eaten as a staple in South India

2. **kaapis:** South Indian filter coffee served in small brass cups

I searched far and wide for a spark of inspiration. In the mornings, I walked among paddy fields and wove past cows through cycle gap *sandhus*[3]. In the evenings, I scrounged under the bridges of bone-dry water canals brimming with cast out refuse and the refused outcaste. I combed through the multitude of temples, some dusty and decrepit, and others ancient but renewed with a fresh coat of neon paint. I even mustered the courage to visit the ever bustling TASMAC[4] of bawdy men and drunken fights. Despite my best efforts, my search yielded no results, and I was left without a muse.

Dejected, I sat down one night and stared at the blank white screen of my computer. In vain, I attempted to break my writer's block, but words refused to flow. The hands of the clock ticked ever closer to midnight and lulled my consciousness towards a sleepless dream.

Lost in thoughts, my gaze drifted across the rented room I'd begun to call home until something caught my attention. Something carefully hidden atop the loft, pushed deep enough inside that you wouldn't notice it at

---

3. **sandhus:** An alley between short buildings with only enough space for a cycle or a cow

4. **TASMAC:** Tamil Nadu State Marketing Corporation which holds a monopoly over all alcohol sales in the state

first glance. A long bundle covered by a cloth so I could hardly make out its shape. Was it an object of importance that the house owner had kept as a memory of a forgotten time? Tomorrow, I would ask the old *paati*[5] who lived downstairs. But in the barren plains of my imagination, acute curiosity took root and propelled me into action.

Ignoring my screaming intuition, I pulled up a chair and hoisted myself atop the loft. I had to crawl on my arms and knees to reach the interior depths of the cavern 'til I reached the misshapen lump of cloth. Gingerly, I lifted the cover. I sneezed, unearthing dust that appeared to have gathered over several centuries. As my vision came into focus, I was astounded by what I saw before me. Wrapped up in a tattered floral bed sheet lay the most beautiful veena I'd ever laid my eyes on. From head-to-toe, the five-foot-long *rudra veena*[6] was a symphony of ivory and honeyed wood. Even in the semi-darkness, it seemed to glow with a light of its own. Painstakingly, I brought the Veena down, and it almost felt like the instrument weighed more than I did.

---

5. **paati:** Grandmother, but also used as a term of respect for an older lady

6. **rudra veena:** An ancient vibrating string instrument used in Carnatic and Hindustani Classical Indian music

In the fluorescence of the tube lights, the White Veena was even more magnificent. Every inch of the musical device was covered in intricate carvings and rivulets of gold. From the top of the twin resonators, concentric circles of petals bloomed and grasped gigantic pearls. The glistening *kodams*[7] were made of several pieces of carved ivory with veins of gold interlocking each individual shard into one whole. Atop the onion domes, sinuous lines of a raging river cascaded down the hazel shaft of the Veena, ending in milky waves. On either side of the Veena, gnarled knots of arthritic fingers twisted around six snowy pegs that protruded like flowers. Above it lay the heavy head of the Veena, which was unlike anything I'd ever seen.

Where I'd expected a dragon head spitting fire, I saw instead the visage of a woman. A block of white and gold sculpted into the shape of a beautiful maiden's face. A woman who bore empty eyes and held her mouth wide open. I couldn't tell if she was singing or screaming. Her hair spilled in curls down the neck of the Veena and transformed into the strings of the instrument. I noticed only then that the black cords were broken and coiled. The alabaster frets on the caramel-coloured wood of the

---

7. **kodams:** The carved and hollowed resonator at the end of the plucked string instrument

shaft looked forlorn without its strings in place. Despite the defect, I could almost swear I heard the faint hum of melody trembling through its severed boughs. I stared at the masterpiece 'til the sun rose and the rooster crowed, and I fell asleep curled around my muse.

With my nose wedged inside a potential story, I went in search of valid sources. I began with the sweet *paati* who lived downstairs and had kindly rented her room to me.

"A white veena, you say?" She wheezed heavily into the *thundu*[8] draped over her nightie. "I don't recall any white veena in the loft. It's not mine. Are you sure you found it in your room?"

I assured her I had very much found it there. "Maybe it belonged to the previous owners of the house?"

"Ah! Maybe, maybe!" She shifted towards me, her massive size straining dangerously on the easy chair. "You see ma, I came into this house only recently. My son lives in America-va, he said *amma*, you need a nice big house.

---

8. **thundu:** A thin cotton towel

My *chellam*[9] bought this big house all for me..."

She continued for a while longer about all the achievements of her beloved son, while I impatiently but politely steered her conversation towards the object of my interest.

"The previous owners were very famous," she said. "Have you heard of Rudhra and Dhwani? World famous classical—Carnatic—music performers. You also listen to Carnatic, no? They perform at the Big Temple every *Margazhi*[10], and people from all over the World come to Thanjavur to see their performance! Rudhra plays the veenai and Dhwani sings. Oho, such divine music!"

"That makes sense. The Veena must be theirs. I would like to return it to them. Do you know where they are now?"

"I don't know, ma..." The old lady lowered her voice and leaned in close. "It was a bit of a scandal, you see. The wife Dhwani ran away with her co-singer Prasanna. *Paavam* Rudhra. He was depressed for weeks after that. Never even

---

9. **chellam:** A term of endearment

10. **Margazhi:** A tamil month (around December) dedicated to spirituality and the pursuit of cultural activities in the form of artistic displays, musical processions, dance performances in temples

stepped out of the house. He stayed inside all day playing his veena the whole time. After that, he also took off. The broker let us buy this house for pretty cheap rates."

"Do they have family here that I can talk to?"

"They were orphans. They had no one. No family, no children, nothing. It is very sad. They didn't tell anyone anything. They carried only the last shreds of their dignity and disappeared."

"Thanjavur is their hometown?"

"Of course, they grew up here only, in the *agraharam*[11] around the temple. Their Carnatic guru lives there. An old veena maker who cared for Rudhra like his own. Poor man must be heartbroken. What a tragedy... No point in these old stories. You tell me, ma, where this Veena is? I'll give it to Ali Bhai, who runs the antique store. It'll fetch me a good price, I think."

"No, no, please! I think it's too important to give it away. Let me see what I find, and I'll let you know."

---

11. **agraharam:** The dwelling surrounding a temple occupied in the ancient days by the Brahmins in charge of maintaining the temple.

That night, I laid the groundwork for my research. My deep dive into the town's archives revealed that the young couple had been at the peak of their musical career. There were nasty rumours at the bottom of the gossip column about the relationship between the wife and her lover, but it was only speculation and generally dismissed. All three of them—Rudhra, Dhwani, and Prasanna—were missing. But there was no mention of their disappearance or their current whereabouts. That seemed to be a secret reserved for those it belonged to.

I couldn't let that stop me from tracking them down. Posting pictures of the Veena and the couple on social media and my friend circles, I began on a desperate quest for leads. The needles of time turned in circles as I devoured videos of their concerts. Dhwani was the embodiment of pure elegance and subtle mischief. Rudhra was the dark deity capable of wreaking havoc on anyone who dared to harm her. They were both blessed with the talent of celestials.

As my eyes glazed over and rolled up in their sockets, it struck me that the head of the Veena bore a striking likeness to Dhwani. I snapped up and stared at the unmistakable resemblance between the two. I had no doubt that Rudhra had built the Veena as an homage to his wife. What story did I hope to discover at the end of my wild goose chase? Could it truly be worth pursuing relentlessly? I wanted to clear the fog of mystery around the disgraced musicians, but I feared the fog was beginning to seize me instead.

The hyper-realistic countenance upon the Veena teared up and shed blood from its eyes. They dripped and dropped on the mosaic floor, adding to its chaotic design. The ruby liquid pooled and ran over my toes. Transfixed, I watched as her chalk lips moved and sang. A melody swam towards me in Dhwani's voice. It paralyzed my bones, rooting me to the spot.

Uncontrollable tears leaked down my cheeks and left a wet path down my neck. I unstuck my hands and wiped them across my face. My fingers came back bloody. Like the mirror of Dhwani, my emotions squeezed and bled. Dhwani turned towards me and croaked, *"Will you let me sing?"*

I awoke with a start. The murmur of a forgotten song echoed in my ears. My obsession was beginning to addle my mind, but sleep eluded me for the rest of the night. As morning arrived, I itched to leave the house despite my bloodshot eyes and the ringing in my ears.

Along the bare bones of the Cauvery with its trash piled high, I went in search of the old veena maker by the *agraharam*. My thoughts mirrored the plastic bag that drifted and found itself caught in brambles, which ripped it to shreds. Red dust covered the brambles. Red plants, red sand, and red walls glowed under the red sun.

My fingers trailed along the uneven facade and gathered the dust of ages past and followed the ancient brick wall that rose ten feet high. Maybe they, too, held secrets no one asked about. I only asked because I wanted to return the Veena. I had no intention of keeping it. A deep part of me ached to hear it play. A longing to see the Veena fixed and hear it sing once before I had to return it.

One step at a time. Red dust rose as my feet crunched on red gravel.

I reached the *agraharam*, and the old part of the town came into view. I walked down the street, hugging the walls of the temple with its low-lying houses and columned homes where upper caste men gossiped and communed. Not a lot seemed to have changed since the old days. Ancient air still hung heavy, hot, and oppressive. Ancient music of the Gods blew softly on the breeze. The strings of a veena pulled at me like a siren's song draws a desperate sailor. I approached the dwelling, which was the source of divine music. On the *thinnai*[12] outside, a gnarled old man sat smoking a *beedi*[13] .

"What do you want?" he asked in a gruff voice.

"Are you *Kalaimamani* Naradaseshan?"

"Yes."

"I heard you build the best veenas in Thanjavur," I began hesitantly.

"Pfft! I build the best veenais in the world. There is no one better."

"I have a veena with broken strings. I would like to fix it. It is made of ivory and wood—"

"No way! Real veenais are only made of the oldest, tallest and best jackfruit trees. Even bamboo or rosewood. Sometimes if you go to these cheap veena makers, you'll even find sawdust. But impossible to build a good veenai out of ivory. Waste. Improper Sound. There's no point fixing a veena like that. Worthless showpiece. I'll show you what a perfect veenai looks like..."

The old man proceeded to lecture me passionately on the art of making veenas. After I listened to him for a few

---

12. **thinnai:** A sort of veranda on a raised platform in front of a traditional South Indian home

13. **beedi:** A mini hand-rolled cigar wrapped in leaf and tied with string

hours, and he gave me a tour of his music school, I finally broached the topic that marinated in my mind.

"Veenai Rudhra learned to play the veena here?"

Instantly, his demeanour changed. The wizened lines on his face smoothed over. His eyes were glazed as a look of adoration came over him.

"Learned? I brought him up! He is my son! He grew up in these very walls. See that pillar there? That is where he sat, the very first time he picked up a veenai. A small boy of four or five years, wrestling with a gigantic veenai. It was almost laughable! But the minute his fingers touched the veena..." He released a deep sigh of satisfaction. "He was a natural. Born to play the veena. That is why we named him Rudhra—after the rudra veena and the intensity that drives his talent. When he plays the instrument, it's just him and the music. He disappears into a world of his own."

I nodded my agreement, but the old man didn't notice. He was held captive by the ghosts of his own past.

"Rudhra hates his name. He said it reminded him of the angry God, which is funny because Rudhra himself doesn't possess a single angry bone in his body! He is the epitome of patience. My best student. I even taught him my art of making veenais. He was the best at that too, but he never made veenais for anyone else. Only built them for his own personal use. He had a large jackfruit grove at the back of his home that he cared for lovingly. With those, he created first class, top rate veenai. That is why his music is so special. No one makes the veenai like him and no one can play it like him. He uses the rudra veena for Carnatic music, mind you, not Hindustani. He plays Hindustani, too, even Western classical! The veenai plays itself for him. That is the gift Rudhra possesses."

He closed his eyes, and his back hunched. In the growing shadows of the twilight, he looked rather frail and miserable.

"You must miss him a lot," I ventured, and he nodded wordlessly. "Do you know where he is now?"

"No," he said despondently. "He didn't tell me before leaving. It's been a few years now, but he will come back soon, I know. He'll come back for me. I am sure."

"What about his wife, Dhwani? Were you familiar with her?"

"Thoo! *Odugaali punda*[14]!" Red flashed in his eyes, and he spat a foamy ball of phlegm on the ground. "Don't ever mention her name to me. She ruined my son. Distracted him from his art, broke his heart, and killed his career! It

---

14. **odugaali punda:** An expletive that roughly translates to "runaway bitch," as in an orphan

makes my blood boil to think of that whore who cheated my son and ran away with another bastard."

I took my leave in haste, realising I'd touched a sensitive nerve. My gut told me it wasn't wise to bring the White Veena to this abandoned old man. I was desperate for the restoration of the Veena, but not enough to risk damage to it.

When I returned to my temporary refuge, I didn't directly go to the Veena like I was compelled to. Instead, I gravitated towards the unkempt grove of aged jackfruit trees. Something about the old veena-maker's discourse on the making of the instrument made me think about the trees that had birthed them. I walked past prickly green fruits bursting at their seams, not knowing where I was headed.

The moment my eyes locked on the tree in my path, I knew it was the one burdened with the secrets I sought. Taller and more ancient than the rest of the trees, it bulged and curved like a dancer in flight. I let my fingers trail the lacerations wrought across its ashy surface. Like my hands had unleashed a torrent, red sap oozed from the wound and spilled over my fingers. Immediately, I withdrew, rubbing my hands vigorously. The scar stopped bleeding, and my hands were sticky from the sap that looked dirty white and very normal.

Before I could process the tricks my eyes had played on me, a jackfruit much larger than my skull detached from the tree and fell right beside me with a crimson splatter. I flinched as it missed crushing my bones by a mere inch. The jackfruit had cracked open and spilled scarlet flesh, flinging its nauseatingly sweet smell into the air. I stepped away from it.

Red mud squelched under my feet as blood ran over my toes.

I blinked and shook my head. The jackfruit was a regular yellow fruit. The muddy water was not any stickier than it should be. My faculties were betraying me. I told myself I wasn't going to read into random occurrences. I needed to sleep. But try as I might, Nidra Devi[15] had deemed me unworthy yet again, and I allowed Dhwani's song to ravage my mind through the night.

---

15. Nidra Devi: The Hindu Goddess of Sleep

I wandered down the sandbank between green, water-laden fields. The wind played with the wide leaves of the palm trees surrounding the paddy fields. The key to unravelling the entire story seemed to lie with the mystery of Prasanna. While Rudhra and Dhwani had no other family, it hadn't been too difficult for me to track down Prasanna's family. I dared to hope despite my failures so far. A teasing tune of breathless promise blew across the back of my neck, and I thought I heard a veena humming merrily.

At the humble Thanjavur home, I had expected to meet Prasanna's parents and instead found the man himself lounging atop a *kaithu kattil*[16] in his *lungi*[17]. Under the pretext of working on an article about the heritage of Carnatic music in Thanjavur, I introduced myself and was promptly invited into their home.

His wife was polite and looked nothing like the pictures of Dhwani I had seen. While Dhwani possessed the unearthly glow of a leashed goddess, this woman was a homely, conventional housewife full of smiles, with her

---

16. **kaithu kattil:** A cot made of palm fiber ropes woven over a simple wooden frame

17. **lungi:** A coloured and patterned full-length skirt worn casually by South Indian Men

hair oiled, braided, and tied with a red ribbon. Their toddler clasped the mother's feet, hiding under her skirt and sneaking looks at me. They were friendly people, and small talk wasn't difficult.

"Were you a part of Veenai Rudhra and Dhwani's troupe a few years ago?" I asked.

Prasanna hesitated before answering, "I was. Would you like some coffee?"

"No please, I am okay."

"I insist," he said and gestured at his wife, who promptly turned and entered the kitchen. The child in the oversized *banian*[18] glared at me and scurried behind her, her *pallu*[19] held tightly in its fist.

"What was it like to work along with them?"

"It was a different time back then. We travelled a lot and did many concerts. We devoted our lives to singing for the Gods. I had no time for a home or a family. Now I get to spend time with my beautiful wife and child, living the family life."

"Did you consider Rudhra and Dhwani to be your family?"

---

18. **banian:** Cotton vest worn by men in India

19. **pallu:** The loose end of a saree draped over the shoulder

"In more ways than I could count, they were family to me. I had no family name to make a mark in the Thanjavur music scene. I am just a farmer's son, not even the right caste. But they saw my talent. Dhwani always said she could see a bit of her in me. They supported me and they helped me grow. For that, I will always be grateful to them."

"What happened then?"

"I am not sure… I will never be sure what actually happened. I couldn't continue singing without them, so I just retired. My father passed away, and I needed to get back to my farm. I have a family now, and they are my responsibility."

I prodded Prasanna further. "I need to get in touch with both of them for my article, but I am unable to trace their contact details. I was told you are their closest contact?"

"No, I am sorry. I don't know where they are right now."

His wife brought us a fresh cup of Kumbakonam Degree Coffee along with plates of *murukkus*[20] and *chandrakalas*[21].

"Bring us *vadais*[22], please," Prasanna instructed her, and she returned to the kitchen.

---

21. **chandrakalas:** A traditional Thanjavur deep-fried sweet filled with khoya and shaped like a half-moon

I protested. "Please—"

His voice turned hostile. "Why do you think I know what happened to them?"

"I heard Dhwani eloped with you. Clearly that isn't true, so you must know what happened."

"Why must I know?! How many people do you think have asked me this question? Even if hundreds of people ask, it will not change my answer. I don't know where she is, and I don't know what happened to her. She probably ran away, and I don't blame her! Her husband was a menace, and she was bound to take action someday."

"She had reason to run away? Was Rudhra being abusive to Dhwani?"

Prasanna closed his eyes and massaged his temples with his fingers. The smell of dough being fried in hot oil wafted from the kitchen, accompanied by sizzling sounds echoing in the silence of the room.

"I've known Rudhra and Dhwani for over a decade, even before they got married. Dhwani was always kind, and she oozed warmth and sunshine. Rudhra... He looks rather stoic, but that's only because he does not know how to express his emotions. Nevertheless, they were the best at what they did. They were the ultimate power couple. I'll admit, I was even jealous of their relationship. But neither of them had eyes for anyone else. They were totally in love and never spent time apart. Joined at the hip they were.

"But I don't know what came over them in those last few months. They were distant and irritable. Rage and resentment filled Rudhra. Dhwani was at the fringe of frustration, soaking in sadness. She abandoned him one day, and Rudhra snapped. Rumours were already floating around by then, and I was sure Rudhra had heard it too. I tried to visit him to make things clear between us, but he refused to see me. It was obvious I wasn't welcome in their home or in their lives. They went their own way, and I went mine."

"There's something I need to be honest about," I said. "I live in Rudhra and Dhwani's old home with the grove. I think I found a veena that belongs to them. A white veena with the head of a woman. I want to return it to them."

Prasanna's face paled visibly, and he snuck a nervous look towards the kitchen, expecting his wife to walk in at any moment.

"Mr. Prasanna, do you know something about it?"

He wiped the sweat beaded on his forehead. "After I learned Dhwani had disappeared, I visited their house. I knocked many times, but no one opened the door. So I went around the back to the grove. There I saw the wrecked ruins of many veenas. There must have been at least twenty, possibly every single veena Rudhra owned."

Prasanna hesitated, swallowing, and then he said softly, "I was scared for Dhwani. No matter how much I banged on the back door, it remained shut, but I knew someone was inside. I swear I heard the unmistakable harmony of a veena. It sounded mournful, and eerily enough…it sounded like a voice. Dhwani's voice."

A sudden breeze whipped my hair into a frenzy and settled uneasily. "Do you think something happened to her?"

"I don't know," he said, shaking his head. "But I'll never forget the sound of that veena. It was nothing like I'd ever heard in my life. It made me want to break down and cry."

The hair on my arms rose of their own accord. "Do you think it could've been the White Veena I found? Why did Rudhra leave without it?"

"I don't know. This was a mistake. Please leave it alone. Nothing good can come out of this. Don't mention it to anyone ever and don't ask any more questions. There's a reason they've stayed hidden, and maybe that is how it was meant to be. This is stirring up unpleasantness for everyone."

On cue, the thoughtful wife entered, bearing more food, and her smile faltered at the expressions on our faces.

The coffee had gone cold and the hot *vadais* were left untouched as I left their home. There was nothing I could do to find closure here. I had more questions than when I'd begun, but the trail had run cold.

I struggled to process my conundrum. A veena without its strings is like a singer without her voice. But my options had dwindled down to nothing. Even if I couldn't return the Veena any longer, I still wanted to hear it. I needed to put it back together. There was so much I didn't know. I was determined to bring life back into the beast, no matter what it took.

I took it upon myself to fix it myself after a basic YouTube education. I unwound the obsidian strings and strained to uncurl the rest of it over the shaft of the Veena. With a twang, it snapped across my hands and left blood in its wake. I withdrew my finger and sucked on it, tasting iron, salt, and the sickly-sweet juice of a decaying fruit.

My fingers bled as I rewound the string and twisted it into knots over its handle. Beads of liquid garnet fell into the Veena's eyes. Tears of blood streaked across its cheeks, dripping over the varnished clay and marbled snow, dropping on the mosaic floor. With excruciating pain, I fastened each strand until all seven were in place.

Vacant silence hung in the air. Unmoving. Waiting. I plucked a chord. No sound came. Not a single note.

I cradled the White Veena in my lap. I hugged it close. I begged and I pleaded. I wailed and I moaned. The strings quivered and sighed. A melody reverberated through the air—a song so soft and filled with pain. The hair on the back of my neck stood on end as the music wrapped around me, gentle and tight. A soft voice on the breeze sang to me. It sang like the strings that played. Slowly and intensely. It told me the story I wanted to hear. It pulled at my heart. My throat clenched. Cold tears welled up and flowed freely.

The story of these lovebirds began less than half a century ago, when Rudhra and Dhwani were just children running down the dusty red streets of Thanjavur. They'd been in love for as long as they'd known each other. As toddlers, they played *pallankuzhi*[23] while the unforgiving sun beat down on their sweaty backs. But as they grew into

---

23. **pallankuzhi:** A traditional mancala game played with cowry shells, seeds, or carved pebble

teenagers, the silence between them stretched like the pause before a *charanam*[24].

Every time Dhwani walked down the road to draw water from the well, she passed by Rudhra's house as he sat on the *thinnai* and worked. They shared smouldering gazes laden with longing. Rudhra's lean muscles flexed as he whittled jack tree wood. Dhwani's hips swayed like the Thanjavur doll. Rudhra nodded at her, producing a tinkling laughter out of Dhwani's lips. Her voice rose, and she broke into a sweet melody and sang to her heart's content.

When Rudhra heard her, every strand of hair on his body stood up on end, all the heavenly bodies aligned and the earth below his feet trembled as the Periya Kovil[25] itself bent in reverence to her. Whenever he tried to talk to her, he could never find his voice.

One fine day, she walked over to his *thinnai* and disrupted his focus on the veena he was carving. "Don't you think we'd make an impressive pair if we performed together at the temple? You play your veena, and I'll

---

24. **charanam:** The chorus section of a classical Carnatic song

25. **Periya Kovil:** The most famous monument of Thanjavur; the Brihadeeswara Temple built in 11th Century AD

sing." After all, she was the one with the voice in their relationship.

With that, they fell in love over and over again, romancing across temple steps as their joy echoed through the music halls. Inevitably, the celebrity couple married each other at a rather simple wedding attended by all the important people in the Carnatic music field.

The first time they made love, Rudhra trailed his finger down her back, the pale whiteness of her curves pressed against the hard planes of his. She inhaled the scent of jackfruit soaking his dark skin and murmured in his ears, "You smell like my most favourite thing in this universe, and now I smell like you. You and I are one. I promise we shall never be apart."

At long last, they bought a large mansion with a jackfruit grove. Rudhra needed to fell the trees to carve his veenas, and his dear wife indulged in the sweet fruits that she loved so much. Their own little paradise that smelled like jackfruits.

But trouble in paradise always seeps in slowly, like varnish through the cracks in wood. A chip wedged into their life in the form of a young man, Prasanna. The singer who performed along with Dhwani had become quite good at extracting musical laughter from Rudhra's lovely wife.

"Do you know what Prasanna thinks? He says I should start singing solo at concerts and try *villupaatu*[26] and *Harikathas*[27]! Don't you think that would be amazing?! I can try out new things for myself!" Dhwani gushed.

This was not the first time his wife had gone on about Prassana.

"Oho, are you getting tired of the old? Our act together isn't enough for you?"

"No, of course not, dear! We'll still keep performing. Our story is one for immortality," she said soothingly, laying her hand over Rudhra's arm.

Rudhra retracted it like her touch had burnt him. "Don't mask your wicked intentions with sweet words. My veena concert is nothing without your voice. What do you expect me to do without you?"

Rudhra was of two minds. As much as he was Prasanna's friend, he could not deny the acidity he felt. Envy burned like coal in the pit of his stomach, but he

---

26. **villupaatu:** A form of musical storytelling practised in Tamil Nadu where the singer uses a musical bow to narrate mythological and social stories to simple tunes

27. **Harikathas:** Another form of storytelling in which parts of Hindu mythology are explored and analysed, accompanied by songs and music

refused to acknowledge it. He neither blamed Prasanna nor Dhwani, but himself for not being able to process his emotions.

As the days passed, the crack widened, and the arguments deepened.

Dhwani was never one to let her desires slip away. She couldn't help herself. "I want to do more! I want to try different styles. I don't want to do the same thing every single time. You have established your expertise with the veena and explored the entire range of what you can do. But I am still singing the same Carnatic songs. There's so much more that I haven't discovered yet! I feel like a child looking out at all the things I want to do with my music, and I am holding back."

"Am *I* holding you back? Aren't you satisfied with me allowing you to sing? What more do you want? Half the men in this town wouldn't dare allow their wives the freedom I allow you. Don't you think you are being too selfish? Maybe it would be better if you stopped performing for a while."

With that, he silenced her voice, and she never spoke again. He went on to travel and perform as he pleased, while she drifted under house arrest like a ghost. An empty shell of the person she used to be.

As the silence settled into permanence, she couldn't take

it any longer. She tied a saree around her favourite jackfruit tree, wrapped it around her vocal chords, and hung herself.

When at last Rudhra returned home, he found his wife swaying free with the wind. He cut her down with tears rolling down his cheeks as he accepted he would never hear her sing again. He caressed her pale skin, knowing his fingers would never play her like the veena again. He cradled her in his arms and wept quietly.

In the depths of his despair, he demolished every veena he owned. He had no need for music in a world without the woman he loved. In an instant, she'd robbed him of the only joy, light, and life he'd ever known. He screamed 'til his voice ran hoarse. The skies echoed his pain and poured down rain.

Mud splattered under the shovel as he dug a shallow grave to lay her beneath her beloved jackfruit tree. The rain tasted like the salt of his tears, and he longed to lie beside her. Unwilling to return to his empty abode, he slept on the disturbed earth and dreamt of a celestial choir ascending to heaven.

The next day, to his utter shock, he discovered the grave of his wife had sprouted a mature jackfruit tree as old as their love itself—twenty-five years and counting. The new tree bore all the curves of a full woman, laden with heavy fruits that weighed down its boughs like hanging babies.

Reminded of his wife's love for the jackfruit, Rudhra plucked the fruits and took it home. He stripped the prickly green skin and spilled its yellow guts. He dug into the soft flesh and peeled it open.

Instead of a seed, there were pieces of a skeleton entombed within. He recoiled in horror from the bloody fruit.

"What sorcery is this?!"

He couldn't stop himself from shredding each one apart as he continued finding fragments of her embedded within the meaty fruit. A bone here, a tooth there. Locks of her hair were wrapped within the spiky green shell. The scent of jackfruit pervaded into the very molecules that made up their home, and Rudhra smelled her with every breath. It overpowered him, driving him insane. Feverishly, he ripped apart fruit after fruit until he'd found the entire skeleton of his wife rebirthed.

Driven into a rage, Rudhra chopped the whole tree down and dragged its carcass into the house. A trail of crimson sap poured all over the floor like the culmination of passionate slaughter.

"If you won't sing anymore," Rudhra growled at thin air, "I'll *make* you sing for me."

Out of the wood, he carved the skeleton of a delicate veena. He bound the shards of her skull with molten gold and sculpted it into her divine visage. Her vertebral column became the frets across the spine of the veena along which his fingers played. Her limbs were embedded into the frosty river running down the fingerboard. Arthritic knuckles knotted around bone flowers that protruded out of the dead tree. Earthen petals danced over twin swollen bellies made of her ribs and pelvic girdle, distorted and fused together with veins of gold. Piece by piece, he shaped every inch of the White Veena out of her remains. From head-to-toe, the five-foot-long veena was a symphony of ivory and honeyed gold.

The carving progressed for days, and he didn't pause to eat, drink, or sleep. At long last, he added the finishing touch and tied her hair as the strings of the Veena.

The chords snapped in place, and silence echoed in the sickly-sweet air. The strings quivered and sighed. A melody reverberated in his mind, a song so soft and filled with pain. He had barely touched it, and the Veena began playing itself.

The hair on the back of his neck stood as he heard a soft voice on the breeze. It sang like the strings that played. Slowly and intensely, wrapping around him and holding him in place. The symphony drew him in and gravity felt heavier. All the heavenly bodies aligned, and the earth itself trembled in fear. His bloodshot eyes widened. He screamed her name over and over.

But as he held the White Veena in his arms, he succumbed to its sound. It played on and rose into a crescendo. The chords snapped and wrapped themselves around his throat. He clawed at them, his eyes bulging as the Veena slowly strangled the life out of him.

His body fell beside that of his muse.

Rudhra and Dhwani were together again.

ABOUT THE AUTHOR

Aksheeya is obsessed with collecting stories like an old witch hoards crystals. Sometimes, she likes to take you on a trip and offer you these tiny capsules of fantasy to carry in your pocket, infect you with its energy, and challenge your own notion of reality.

linktr.ee/aksheeya

*Thank you for supporting Graveside Press and our authors.
One of the biggest ways you can help is to leave a star rating
or a review wherever you purchased your copy!*

Stay spooky.

Wanna come hang out with the ghouls?
gravesidepress.carrd.co

Stay up to date with Graveside news and exclusive stories.
graveside-press.com

Please note: because this is horror, it should be assumed that the basic horror tropes will apply. These include death, gore, and violence.

suicide

death of a spouse

domestic violence

desecration of a corpse